Up Through the Night

UP THROUGH THE NIGHT

BY

JOCELYN TOMAKA

For:
My friends

TABLE OF CONTENTS

1. The Meat Was All the Rage   2

2. A Sinking Belle   8

3. Human Nature   14

4. I Won   22

5. The Streets of London   28

6. Cleaving Through the Smoke   32

7. Universal Hum   38

8. The First Sunday of Every Month   42

9. Nighttime Cavity   52

10. Put Alex in the Abyss   58

11. Prisoners of War   62

12. When Summer Was Summer   66

13. The Long Man   72

14. Killers   82

15. The Psychic   88

16. Vision Thing   92

17. Soliloquy   100

18. This Time Around   108

19. The Summer Circled Back Around To Us   112

20. 101 Ways to Die in Amsterdam   122

The Meat Was All the Rage

The building was innocuous, as far as being a pre-war construction suited for a large family on the upper floor and a business on the ground, on the corner of an unremarkable suburban street. When I was very small, the top floor was made into apartments, and the ground floor was made a barbershop. I could see the back, upstairs patio from my kitchen window, and I was envious of the residents' sunbathing in the summer. I find it ironic that there are people who resist change because all life is change, and all things change in time, and so did the innocuousness of the rectangular corner building.

I entered into high school that year, and my boyfriend already graduated the year before, so he found a job at the newly renovated innocuous corner building. They made the ground floor into a bar, and although I only ventured in occasionally to bring Jeff a message (—a time before cell phones!) or a personal item he might have forgotten at my place, I saw people coming and going, and he told me stories, so I knew a bit about the joint. The regulars were mostly local

2

bikers and blue-collar guys, trapped, for one reason or another, in a small, suburban enclave in western New York. There was never much trouble from the group, and the owner, Jimmy, was tough as nails. He had a baseball bat that he pounded on the bar if people played absolute crap on the jukebox, but for the more serious affronts, he had his boys. Jeff was not one of these boys, as he was just there to keep the place clean and do the grunt work—his father knew Jimmy, being a bar owner himself, and got Jeff the gig. The rest of the boys who worked there were long and strong, and in no uncertain terms, existed to keep order. I think Jimmy was a bookie, but that makes no difference as to the outcome of the innocuous building.

What everyone knew without a doubt was that Jimmy was stark raving mad. He came from a long line of full-blooded Irishmen who loved sports, Jesus, their families, booze, and rebellion (in that order?), but I think the long line was so convoluted and tainted that by the time it ended with him, his goose was cooked. He made a lot of money and lived in a remote, rural part of town, but his best customers thought his new location for business was very convenient. Our suburb was ideally situated far enough from the ghettos that lined the southern borders of the big city, but not too far into the highbrow suburbs that comprised the hillside havens. Lucky us.

It does not sit very well with me to remember my hometown, now, or to recall the images of my youth—the streets that I knew by heart, in the dark, the sounds of the trains' Doppler calls, the sight of the apartment dwellers sunning on porches—all tainted by the grotesque nature of the happenings at the building on the corner.

The details of how Jimmy and his gang of inhuman, inbred monsters were eventually exposed are not clear to me, as I do not think they were clear to me then. Jeff quit a few months after he started, having gained better employment elsewhere. He complained that the building smelled funny, especially out back, and he did not like working for and with bullies. Jimmy seemed nice enough, but you just never knew when his temper would ignite, and people were always going out of their way to NOT piss him off. The patrons seemed nice enough as well, but there was a sinister undertone to their interactions that made Jeff feel like he was in a lost episode of

Twin Peaks gone sideways. He just laughed at all their jokes, kept his nose out of the restricted areas, and his ears out of hushed, covert conversations, and tried to keep people from complaining if he delivered food to their table too late.

Sometimes, the kitchen staff was nowhere to be found, and Jeff assumed they were out back taking one too many smoke breaks. The odd thing was, whenever he went out back to smoke, they were not there, either. When he asked Jimmy about it, Jimmy explained that they were probably doing inventory in the cooler. The innocuous old building was big enough to store an extended family of Irish immigrants, but not big enough to lose them within. Still, Jeff kept his nose clean and just did what he had to do, with the occasional perk of getting high with the regulars out back, having a few drinks, and eating some of the best burgers in town.

The problem was, the burgers were made from live horsemeat. Turns out, there was a whole section of "out back" that was concealed behind a brick wall, and there were two "machines" installed that Jimmy crafted himself. The horses were restrained by the machines, their blood slowly siphoned out, and their meat cut from them while they still breathed.

The patrons came from all over town for the meat; in turn, they then sold the machines to members of their extended networks outside of town. The meat was all the rage.

Years later, the innocuous building was condemned (I'll say…) and as they were removing bits of it, I got a decent view of the machines. They just looked like pieces of metal fashioned as restraints, but later Jeff told me there were other more tortuous parts of them that had rusted, decayed, and disappeared with time. He said that one of the finer elements acted like miniature forceps around the horses' eyes to keep them open, to keep their terror flowing, as they were slowly dying. He said I absolutely did not want to know how they handled the natural evacuation of the bowels that occurs when any animal dies.

I remember, one chilly Sunday autumn afternoon as I was waiting for Jeff to meet me after work I stood adjacent from the building and could hear indecipherable sounds that made me scared. I thought the boys might be having too good a time with some women who were not as willing. Jeff came screeching around the corner in his 1987 Grand Marquis, having just off-loaded a few patrons who needed rides home, and he stunk of weed and alcohol. We got into a massive fight that night because I swore he knew more than he was letting on, and that bad things were happening, and he might even be protecting people because of his father. Turns out, I was wrong, but it hardly matters. Jeff didn't know anything about the horses. And neither of us knows any more about the rest.

A Sinking Belle

We had twenty-five acres of rolling hills, and beautiful sycamore trees spotted the front yard. A pithy, green pond was back behind the house, slightly stocked, surrounded by endless lines of evergreen trees. Then there were the fields. We were tucked away in a remote farming town where everyone knew your name, but the sprawl of the land allowed you to feel lost whether you liked it or not, and the hills and the fields were everywhere. The main house was up on a small hill about a hundred yards back front the two major county crossroads. The woods and the pond started a hundred yards to the rear of the house, and a vertiginous valley formed adjacent to the guesthouse. The big brown barn stood in between.

Unfortunately, Mr. Earl had passed away five years ago, and his old Chevy pick-up was painfully parked in "the dip," with the hood permanently rusted red into an opened position. I think it was built in the 30's, and the blue paint was barely holding on. I was waiting to press the issue to Mrs. Earl, so we could have the eyesore removed. I was the handyman. I took care of the main house, slept in the guesthouse, and was always treated like family once I started two years previous, discharged from the 82nd for a bullet wound to my gut.

It was an odd family, that's for sure. The numbers had dwindled over the war years. Then again, the war took its toll on everyone. Mrs. Earl lost Mr. Earl to a heart attack, but they both lost their boys to the theater in Europe. This cost Mrs. E her heart, too—her spirit was broken, and she was scatterbrained to a fault. She kind of glided in and out of situations like water. If often seemed to me she was mechanical and lost.

This left the girls. Sister number one lived in town where her job was. We called her Sister Em, and she popped in almost every other day or so with her two hyperactive little kids. Sister number two we called Sister Bea. She was in the family by law; her husband was the oldest brother lost to the last year of the war. They were married in haste because she got pregnant, and now she was stranded with a baby boy. I say stranded because everything she did was towards making a better life for her and her baby, and then moving on. She was a tough cookie and sometimes reminded me of me.

Sister Bea had a stalker. He was a piece-of-work. He was also Mrs. E's favorite person by far; he acted like a "replacement" son. He was her nephew, Mr. Earl's only brother's child who dodged the draft, but lost both his parents in Manila. He took over their farm about eight miles away from us, farther from town. He was inexplicably drawn to Sister Bea as all the boys were at one time or another, but she refused his propositions of marriage politely. He persisted, and Mrs. E resented her for it. I think she was jealous. It all seemed crazy down deep, but it was intensely human nature.

I called her stalker, "The Baron." He was arrogant with a little dose of crude on the side. He was built like a brick shit-house and used to getting whatever he wanted. "What a jack-ass!" I found myself thinking, often. He slapped me on the back like I was his brother, but he didn't mean it unless he was trying to manipulate something out of me. Sister Bea and I were the only ones who could see through his act. We made fun of him, giggling at our own jokes incessantly, yet no matter what, we kept our jokes safe and secret since The Baron was menacing. He was frightening in his mannerisms and his stature, but most intimidating in his ignorance and solipsism. We figured he'd just fade into the distance someday, or we would eventually escape the other way.

As for my feelings for Sister Bea, I just enjoyed every day with her, and never forced the issue that I thought I had to be with her no matter what. I would never force the tides to turn in my favor, and I would never push things; I would never lie more of a burden at her feet than she already had to contend with. And, of course, I was fairly certain she didn't feel the same way. Like I said, she had this inexorable pull, and I was probably just another hapless victim. Then again, she might've felt the same way, and who was I to make decisions that sealed fate? Apparently, that was a job for The Baron, and Sister Bea remembers the beginning of the end better than I do since she was there. She brings it back now:

Clint and I were sitting on the daybed in the back of the house. I was just getting up since it was an exceptionally hot summer morning, and I functioned much better later into the day when things cooled down. Clint must've been up early to try and make the most of his day, since all physical labor at any time outside during the summer was a ridiculous feat of bravery, in my opinion. I hated the summers there on that farm, and every autumn I tried to forget them. Anyway, we were sitting on the daybed while I dressed Albert, and we were laughing hysterically at something I can't recall for the life of me now, but we did that a lot. Clint has such a great smile, its infectious! So, I was taking my time about things, unaware of the movement of time that day, and then The Baron appeared. He walked in through the screen door across the room and was evidently not happy with what he saw. I was immediately aware that it was probably inappropriate in his mind for me to be sitting there with the handyman in my robe clothing my half-naked baby, laughing and carrying on. Plus, The Baron had a thing for me and a thing for conquests, and he was such a wingnut, so of course he was going to be all in a tizzy.

Clint was incredibly cool about the whole situation—he didn't even flinch as he got up and declared, "I better get to mowing that lawn now—bye kiddies." He patted Albert on his fuzzy head and left the way The Baron came in; walked right by him with a gleaming smile and was fluid in his maneuvering.

12

The Baron leaned against the counter, kind of leering at us, chewing on a piece of hay or grass or whatever hick-thing he had a hold of. He watched Clint walk by, and never stopped staring at me. I didn't realize he was moving towards me as he slowly made his way. I thought he'd eventually just pass through towards the kitchen, towards Mrs. E, but instead he stopped in front of me. He stood over me and as I was nervously saying something like hello or how are you all the while trying to figure out why he was acting so strange. Then he pulled out a hunting knife and hacked my index finger on my right hand off.

Human Nature

Henri bought a house. We were all due to celebrate with him at a barbeque he was hosting Saturday evening. There were a few reasons I did not want to go, but it was hardly worth it to try and explain to my friends my absence, so I went, anyway.

Aunt Gertrude also just bought a house, in a neighborhood adjacent to Henri's. Although I tried very hard not to show it because I did not want to alarm anyone, I was concerned that the area might be susceptible to crime moving in, so I limited my questions to just one: *had she researched the crime rates in this new area?* She answered me with sort of a lengthy and outmoded exposition about how people she knew in the neighborhood, and their self-invented hypotheses (almost empirically proven by anecdotes, of course), assured her things were safe. All this rambling made it easy for me to drift off with thoughts of my own.

I was preoccupied with what I dreamt the night before: I was brutally attacked, raped, by a gang of men, who were later apprehended, and I was then able to punish of my own accord. They preyed upon me on a very blustery winter evening, in front of my Mother's home, beneath the orange haze of a street light fighting against the snow and wind. I punished them in the same location but standing in Aunt Gertrude's sunny and green back yard, I could not recall by what means I had laid siege to the pathetic men with their black slits for eyes and patched-up flesh. And the irony was still nagging at me: why did no one see me and save me from their attack? My Mother's boyfriend helped capture the scourge, and mistakenly brought along one of the monsters' child, a boy of seven years old, dirty and belligerent. In this nightmare, I stomped his little head in while the father was forced to look on. The hellish cries were lost to the white blanketed skies.

I couldn't worry about Aunt Gertrude any longer as other worries took the forefront of my mind. Going to Henri's party seemed ironic itself since he only invited me because he still hoped I would be interested in joining him, and he knew I would be forced to face the subversive sneers of some "friends" who loved to gossip about me/Henri and I/everyone else on the planet. Needless to say, I wanted nothing to do with them, but I wanted to appear above their salaciousness, and continue to support Henri, even though I didn't think it wise to buy the house he did at the time he did.

The final reason I did not want to go to Henri's was because I simply did not feel like talking to anyone. I felt disturbed, frightened, vulnerable, and haunted; things just didn't feel right, like the way a hot summer night brought about elation because of some false sense of freedom. When I arrived at Henri's, the smell of roasting flesh covered in a sugary smoke cloud forced me to immediately find the corner furthest away from the bounding, slaying chef, Henri.

Later, then, my Father showed up. I talked to him on the phone earlier this day, for the first time in over a month, and clearly I was upset. I blasted him about forgetting me in exchange for the booze, always having excuses, and lying to me and himself. I wanted to see him more than a jilted lover longs for the capitulation of her deserter, so much that I couldn't help but cry every time I pleaded with him. This time he said that he would just stop by sometime during the night since he lived near Henri's new digs, although I expressed doubt that my old man would be conscious or remember at all.

He was not supposed to be driving. He was exhausted from work and a lack of sleep, and half in the bag, I'm sure. He had such a hard time sleeping, almost all his life, and in retrospect, I see how the insomnia was enough of a disease to beg for relief through alcohol...or death. I suppose that is another part of the reason he drank, besides the drink being a disease itself.

The strange thing about him now was that he was swaying a bit, which he never did, and yet seemed focused upon finding me. I saw him approach down the side of the blue-paneled house, up the gravel driveway, and over to me in my corner by the porch steps. The first thing I said was that he didn't look well at all, and that he should not be driving, and in his defense, he collapsed against me, quickly slouching into my feet.

I am not surprised that no one heard my screaming or saw this tragedy unfurling by the yellow light of the kitchen window. I dragged him a few feet over to the steps and shouted in through the screen door for someone to call an ambulance. Henri was on his way out of the kitchen with a plate of deviled eggs, and he dropped them all as he saw my anguished contortions, and a pale, sleeping man in my grip. The eggs bounced on the dark green shards of grass, leaving trails like pigeon poop. He rushed back inside, leaving the mess, and phoned 911. I saw him dial it, and how he could not stop staring at the face of the phone as he came back down the stairs and began directing me towards the driveway. All sound became echoes and all light became fog as I moved my gaze from Henri's face to my Father's torso: it was moving, he was breathing; I lowered my head against his bony chest and heard the lub-dubbing of his heart. I began to cry quietly and inconsolably, resting my head against his head, begging him not to die.

No one else among the party stirred. Now I felt protected from their watchful stares at the most important hour as I tried to save my Father's life. Finally, some relief.

Henri helped me move Daddy to the edge of the street, even though I felt very strong carrying my weakened love, as if I could save him above all else. The ambulance took forever, of course, and when they finally arrived and pulled Daddy away from me and onto a gurney, the ambulance operators seemed grotesquely delighted that he was only sleeping: exhausted, not unconscious.

I was left staring at the flashing lights as the roaring vehicle turned the corner of Henri's block, my tears drying up, my hearing becoming a void, my eyes struggling to identify my Father's pick-up truck parked alongside the crowded streets. I managed to wrest his keys from his front pocket before they took him, and now, as I moved along the street, I wondered what I would do once I found his truck. Would I rush to his house, ransack it looking for evidence against him, proving to him once of for all that he was killing himself? Would I sleep there, huddled up with the smell of him on his velvety blue and beige cotton sheets, with sounds unfamiliar and menacing to me?

Would I drive the small truck straight through the enormous panels of glass concealing the entrance of the parish hospital, screaming bloody murder, leaving bloodied tire tracks, cursing ever one and everything, offering some nonexistent higher entity my soul in exchange for vengeance? Or would my nightmares convert to encrypted letters of abandonment and eternal suffering, repeatedly recalling that I would never have my Father's love again?

It didn't matter: my Mother found me, pathetic, bouncing off cars, sobbing my way up and down the block, looking for that truck. I saw another ambulance coming our way and asked her if they got lost on their way to the hospital? She said that they did not of course, because my Father died 15 years ago.

I Won

I won $700.00. This is not a terribly large sum, and it felt more like a slap in the face at a crucial moment—even though I was only making toast when I found out. Maybe I was delirious? I cannot find the ticket stub now to save my life, and I know I will need it to prove why $700.00 is missing from the house.

My Grandmother's kitchen was altered to accommodate two scratch-off lottery ticket machines. I assume this happened because of the constant flow of traffic with family and friends, melded with their consummate love for scratch-offs. I am awfully fatigued since we buried my Father yesterday morning, yet I am up almost two days in a row now and unable to sleep. In the back of my mind I have a clear thought of Clark and his dead father: he coped so well; will it ever come back to hurt him as it has hurt me because I am at a critical age? I am beginning to see things the way they truly are now that I have been on my own for a few years, while Clark still believes in benevolence and magical money trees.

This is all I can remember from that time: I went away to school, and came back with the same face, but not the same voice. I slowly heard the right one, then let the wrong one in; I began to live with perpetual paranoia, weighing on me with the knowledge that it would never leave me, especially not in this house.

I used my voice less frequently. I stopped speaking out against things, and began moving away from people, so that at any given time you would find me outside smoking a cigarette, cleaning out my car, or in the basement hanging out. I learned to stay as far below the radar as possible until I figured out why I was now living here, in my aunt's bedroom, and not living with my Mother. I didn't have the courage to ask. My voice just froze when I started the question. It was the strangest thing.

I never saw Clark anymore. The first Christmas I would spend in their house would be next week, and I wondered if he would be there, and what he would say. I was hesitantly hoping he would be the voice of reason to come in and startle me the entire way out of this coma.

Only a few of my friends knew where I was staying, and when they came by, we stayed outside. They could sense that I was not very happy, but they assumed it was because I was still mourning my Father. Oddly, instead of gratitude for the concern, I felt a growing resentment that they were too stupid to figure out just what the hell was going on. Then Gabriel found out where I was, and my time outside grew less and less.

He would climb in through the window, completely fine with letting me work out the current dilemma independently, probably out of respect for me and fear for us being isolated from one another completely. I am sure my Grandmother would have no problem calling that shot. I stopped asking why so long ago, it seemed ancillary. The most important thing was being with Gabe to preserve my remaining clarity and inspiration, because I think I loved him and defying the family in at least some way. Although it was getting more painful every day, to see Gabe slip through the window, and to suffer the whispers of the family in the kitchen.

Turns out more people knew where I was than I expected: Clair called to ask for my help in preparing for a party before

Christmas. I found the phone message in a pile of other small notes, a week too late. I began to believe that they just didn't really care about me, per se, and if I left again, no harm would be done. I needed a plan. Gabe was completely willing to help me, and one night he was so excited I thought he would burst, and that's when I realized why…I was being punished.

I was married, to a man who turned out to be a very bad man, and the family said that they were keeping me safe, but they were actually just pissed off and practicing their version of "damage control." The entire scene poured into my head as if some great levee had given way, and I sobbed the rest of the cold winter night. Gabe was still there in the morning, which he usually is not, and said that we should just leave now. He whispered his words against the frosted panes of glass, leaving traces of white hot breath. The problem was, it was Christmas Eve, and the ENTIRE family would then be riled up. Who knows what they would do?

I will never forget this moment: sitting up in my cotton nightgown, sweating through my head, eyes swollen from the despair, staring through the pain that was in his eyes—I was either REALLY sick, or I had lied to him. Neither of those reasons was good. And I could tell he was agitated. I feared that if he slipped out that window without me, he might not come back. And if he did come back, what would I do? Would it be safe for me to be in his life? Would it be safe for any of us ever again?

I went out to the kitchen and saw the preparations were already at hand for the night's feast. My aunt was already there, of course, to help out. She was currently taking a break, thumbing through some photo albums. They were very old photo albums by the looks of them, and the musty smell of aged paper filled the space around the kitchen table with a strong pull. At first, I looked over my aunt's shoulder, but then I began flipping through a smaller book situated to her right. I slid into the seat next to her, and Grandma came over to talk about which people were who in the monochrome photos, and I couldn't believe I was part of this life. I also could not stop looking, as I saw more modern, familiar faces, and tears of bittersweet longing trailed down my quivering cheeks. Grandma's hands reached over to the book my Aunt was viewing and settled on a man: the man she said was the handsomest man she had ever seen. It was Grandpa, the very one who threw her out a window decades ago in a drunken rage.

I, scared of my own shadow at this point, ran back into my room, and began packing my shit. I was out of there, Gabe, Clark, Christmas Eve, or not.

The Streets of London

The streets of London are eerily quiet near the Queen's Gardens. I expected the teeming sounds and sights would pervade well into a slightly sinister darkness, but with the veil of twilight came the onset of solemnity. A very distinctive looking gentleman approached my friend and me as we walked back towards Westminster, and I assumed he would either want a fag or directions. He brushed by us, just kept walking, and I felt my face flush from my mistake, even though no one else knew of my shortcoming. *How silly of me*, I thought. I turned to look behind me towards his egress, and he met my look: he stopped and turned around. He asked where we were heading, and I promptly replied, "The tube— back towards Victoria Station…" He then invited us to a coffee house around the way and motioned with his head for us to follow. "I can tell you are charming tourists and you must try this local favorite!" Within moments we were seated with him, being charmed and entertained, in an Indian fashion.

I cannot say for certain why we carried on with him into the wee hours of the morning, but another distinctive looking gentleman met up with us before midnight, and he was the equally charismatic brother of the gentleman. There was nothing suspicious about either one of them, and we jokingly inquired as to why they were not out with girlfriends instead of strangers this Friday night? The first gentleman replied with some casual utterance about how life just works out the way it does, and how amusing it all is. My friend and I agreed despite not knowing where the amusement in our situation quite lay, in a fearfully foreboding sort of way.

Regardless of the travesty that thus ensued, I still adore London. I adored it in my childhood daydreams, my adolescent visions, and my young adult excursions; it is an ethereal and everlasting mythic conception. *Screw Paris.*

Our hotel was by the British Museum, and although we did not invite the gentlemen to escort us home, they were there with us waiting in queue outside the museum for a special early morning exhibition. It seemed to be highly anticipated and rousingly popular since all kinds of people swarmed the stairs, and were intent upon getting in. There was something hypnotic about the gentlemen with us—who decided to queue with us; they fit into a formula wherein London was the enchanter, and the museum was a reaction to a catalyst, and they were the metamorphosis.

A modern-day coliseum is what I remember next: benches and hallways and stairs and hidden passages all around us in white marble and black wood. The interior of the museum was huge, and filled with people, with barely a meter to spare. I made eye contact with my distinctive gentleman, who then made me blush, and I was again flush with fear: *why were we here?* He did not return any indication of acknowledgement. We made our way through the exhibits, but he kept disappearing on errands of some sort. Each time he returned to my side he reassured me there was nothing to fear. I think those are famous last words in London.

In front of Rembrandt's innumerable self-portraits, I overheard my gentleman talking with his brother, and while families were playing with their children and people were stirring about being warm and hungry, etc., I panicked. We all seemed to be taking shelter. And no one else seemed to feel my fear. Everyone about me, including my traveling companions, was calm and content with the surrounding *non-* situation. I insisted to myself, that I must be paranoid. *Get it together! It isn't as though the Waffen is coming.*

No—no Germans, only distinctive, scientifically fictitious gentlemen planning to sort the city out. Maybe there was something "English" going on, and we were ignorant tourists—a thought that once would have been disconcerting but was now a suggestion of sanity against a backdrop of betrayal. *Was this Armageddon?* The gentlemen had schemes and shifting eyes, and I felt a need to save us all.

The betrayal played on with such ambiguity I could never articulate the scene with any decent semblance of recollection. I informed my friend of the seemingly awful terrorism of the distinctive gentlemen, and she refused to believe me; she sensed nothing of the sort. She refused to see the obviousness of my panicked exterior contrasting the chilling, secretive demeanor of the gentlemen. I excused myself from Rembrandt, my palms sweating along the rails, and rushed out into the crowds of people trying to get in. I was blind in my heading, rushing over sidewalks and pavement, away from the sound of the bomb that went off far behind me.

Cleaving Through the Smoke

The light filters through the sheers in the bathroom, white and peppered with pink flower petals, falling. It is an ominous light, as if a thunderstorm is rolling in and snuffing out any acuity in its path with comforting obscurity. I love being in this room. And today, I am filling glass vases, sorting out red carnations, half-dead roses, long, green leaves and stems, and baby's breath, from a pile of foliage on the toilet top. I am hovering over the white porcelain sink, in front of the mirrored medicine cabinet built in 1955, the year my Grandparents moved the family in.

The water surges to the middle of a bowed-out glass, and I arrange the pickings to the brim with bursting beauty. Once filled, I set them aside on the carpeted toilet lid, and reach for another vase: there are two filled, and I look to fill three more, the next a green, skinny cylinder, which barely fits a stalk of plump, mossy leaves, heavy with the weight of water. I wonder if it will tip the entire vase over and think that perhaps I should dry the heavy moss, but it looks confidently soothing hanging lower than the rest, so I take my chances.

I walk my fingers around the plastic shelf space quartered above the toilet, searching for the bottom of the last vase. I cannot find any more glass cylinders, instead cautiously selecting an oriental, white polished ceramic urn. My mind seems a little tripped-up by breaking the linear symmetry of a long, translucent soldiering of glass-encased flora, but the urn is all I have left, so I have to settle.

I wish I could stay in the tiny bathroom; I love the oak door next to laundry chute. There are butterflies in my stomach as I carry the vases out, two by two into the blue walled room across the hall. I pay no mind to whomever might be in the house, continuing the silence and the softness of my task, and setting up the vases on different surfaces throughout the small, blue room. The first vase I place on the nightstand; the second, on the sewing table next to the closet, the third, on the dresser, and then I lose count. I am distracted.

The light is the same in this room as it is in the bathroom, and I can only very slightly make out the form of the crying woman seated on the bedside across from the window. The sound is a mournful lull, full of defeat and despair. Her tears come timidly, with her voice buried deep in crumpled tissue and cupped hands. My brain is washed over in a reactive, chaotic melding of emotions.

I am afraid she will see the flowers; I do not understand this fear, I do not understand her pain, and I do not understand what to do with myself in this moment. Like looking for a glass bud vase, I hesitate to select the emotion that will drive my actions in the next few moments, a response typically carried out unconsciously. We are two characters in the likes of this twilight zone, somewhere in between things. Her weeping pulls at the core of me, and as I sit down with her, I take her into my arms. I whisper, "Shhh, what's the matter now?"

She begins to pull back, shivering a little, and sniffing in for some breath to speak. She looks at me, eyes red and wet, and beautifully shiny in blue. Then she collapses again, her face covered in shame, in a tiny, hysterical voice squeaking out, "I am crazy; He thinks I am crazy, and I am!"—as if to say she is lost—all is lost.

I think I should tell her to leave. I know there is a part of him that wants her, and is trying to ensnare her, desperate to fill the void his displeasure and boredom, ignorance and fatigue has carved out in his endlessly hollow underbelly.

The light turns a more sinister grey, and I notice the vases are still where I placed them, but ravaged, reduced to a third of their former glorious capacity, tattered by photoelectric claws. As the woman weeps further in my arms, my confusion and fear replace my sympathy, and a demand begins to assert itself, echoing from the bowels, saying *choose*.

With a recovered face I wonder what has happened to my vases? Did *he* get in, between us and our short time here, where we did not turn our backs to the door, and reduce everything?

Deep beneath my internal disarray there is that clarity: I simply want to burn the whole house down. I want to blow it all away. But he has the power, and his absolute power is self-serving, without fail, far away from resolution and peace. This is the house that killed my Father and this is the room that kept me awake, and my Mother is the woman they punished, and the bed sheets are soaked in a startled sweat.

I hold the woman tighter, and whisper back to her that she is crazy, but it is necessary and natural; she is beautiful, and now it is time for us to leave.

Universal Hum

Up again before my body, my mind piecing together a most detailed and tactical dream, back in my Grandmother's house.

None of the original inhabitants remained save the old furniture: sleek, shiny aluminum legged chairs and tables with exaggerated pastel vinyl in blues and greens; hideously patterned exhausted sofas and loveseats, tarnished beige and brown with dying orange flowers; and the classic "Hi-Fi" stereo record player, which remained in the basement— once it played The Clash and The Police for me. Always the upper living spaces: the kitchen, the dining and sitting rooms, were reserved in their invariable singularity as opposed to the basement, which was respite during the hot summer days, and chilling at night, haunted.

The people I currently call my family in my waking life lived in this disallowing house in my dream—and back there, they grew tired of me. All the energy I possessed burned them right through. They all moved sluggish and sideways, their eyes casting vacant looks towards whomever approached them—as I witnessed it, moving in and out of the frame. Eventually, I barely excited a response from them at all, and we moved on seemingly separately planes of existence.

The woman of the house, with a weary, betraying look, asked that I remove myself to the basement for good. For the tenth time in ten years, I relocated my parceled belongings, dragging myself down the linoleum stairs—not without question, but without a fight: I must be used to this. The anxiety and despondency pushed more easily aside by the acceptance of my reluctant circumstance, and my honed, coarse mechanism of survival.

I grasped onto the furniture. I rearranged it piece by piece although I scarcely moved each item more than a foot in proximity to its infant position. I had something of a semi-circle around the Hi-Fi in the end. All that was left to move was the pull-out sofa, the most uninviting character in this dance.

I would never fit it.

There was nothing available to make it softer for me to lay on; I might never have rest again under these conditions! And there was nowhere else to go albeit my slowing waking mind could not reason why, as there were windows and doors on two sides of the chiaroscuro ensconced room. I would challenge myself to resolve this dilemma; now, I would listen to the noises from the people moving above me, lamenting.

But it didn't work out this way at all.

Something unrecognizable flipped my switches and turned my head away from the fortuitous fabric leviathan, back towards the record player's remarkably hospitable alien green light that read, "ON."

I pushed the button.

An extension of me, the sound grew wild, filled everything up, and I forgot a little about those above me, who hid in near-silence and shadows, thinking they could ever truly live their lives away from electricity, fearful they would burn. But I knew differently: I danced that dance before, too.

The First Sunday of Every Month

He beat her the first Sunday of every month. He was resentful that she was only an aspiring actress while he was a custodian of the local college. The first Sunday of every month, she was off. She spent the whole week off, and if her lazy ass was out working, he might not have to teach her a lesson. You see, he hated his job. He was dignified, and his contribution was necessary, but he knew the hordes of people racing past him each morning did not appreciate him. He needed to teach all of them a lesson, too, but he was so busy at the moment; he just did not have the time.

The beating was not too bad—most of the bruises were kept to her scalp or her torso where they would be undetectable by anyone else. He used his fists, and then he forced himself on her—on their sagging old mattress with stained white sheets, eventually passing out. She stopped crying on those nights, a long time ago. She would get up, treat her wounds, and smoke a cigarette, waiting for the morphine to kick in strong enough to put her to sleep. Every first Monday of the month, he would come home with flowers and take her to the street vendors for dinner. He was always so remorseful, fearful she would leave him, and this just confused him even more. He suspected maybe he should spend time teaching other people lessons, because she never seemed to learn; maybe she should be an exception?

She did not think she was going to be an actress anymore. She did not tell him, but she spent the time she was supposed to be auditioning and training, and occasionally, working, at Rigley's joint, scoring up whatever eased her. She looked in the mirror and saw tired eyes and wilting skin, a rose dying on the vine. Her pixie-cropped dark blonde hair lacked the sheen it once had, and her sparkling green eyes appeared dull and fading. Her milk-white skin was a hollow sort of yellow, and her thin, pink lips, gray. She was as thin as a rail, and her unusually small clothing barely hung to her wasting frame. No one intervened. There was no one to intervene. She simply told her agent that Nick had a job that supported both of them well-enough that she could go back to art school. Her only art now was waiting to die.

She thought that if anyone ever loved her, they would tell her to leave Nick, but the problem was that he was the only one to ever love her. She was confused, as well. One time, he was burning her thigh with a match, and she kicked him. He laughed and stopped burning her, so she thought about fighting back.

Nick was on his best behavior the past month—he seemed like a new man! He was unusually kind to her and started talking about having a family. He flushed all of her birth control pills down the toilet and took her every night in an effort to make his dreams a reality. He stopped chastising her for not bringing in the same amount of money she used to (when she began to find real work) because he decided she would have to quit to raise the baby anyway. She asked him where the necessary additional funds would come from once they had an extra mouth to feed, and he stared at her, long and hard. He got that look in his eyes, like a storm moving in over a prairie, dark, fast, and mean. This time, however, instead of smacking her, he pinched himself in the stomach and reassured her that he was on top of that detail. All she had to do, he insisted, was learn how to be a mother. She started praying to God that he or she—or whatever God was—would take her. She was even willing to go to Hell.

Nick's plans were put into motion on a humid July evening, as they students filtered out of the school. The dean was having an affair with his assistant, and his wife and three kids would not be happy to hear about it. Nick showed the dean the pictures he took when he caught them having sex in the pool house last month, and the dean was very willing to start paying Nick an extra $1,000 a month to keep his mouth shut. Nick thought that was fine lesson for the dean to learn, and a fine way to make extra money. Each first Friday night of the month, Nick would wait for the dean outside the pool house and get his money. This Friday night he decided to collect money from the assistant, too, and a little something extra—he wanted one of her toes. He would keep it on ice and should either of the two adulterers decide to break the deal with him, Nick would rock that town with such a scandal they wouldn't know what hit 'em.

The problem was, the dean showed up with the chief of police and some additional muscle, all of which Nick witnessed from his perch on the great elm tree adjacent to the pool path. He felt the sweat begin to collect under his baseball cap, soaking his forehead, and he scurried down the massive tree, panicked and pissed. He thought he would kill all those motherfuckers. He leaped from the last limbs of the tree, and his camera smashed to bits when it slammed against the brick pathway, falling from his weakened grip. Nick could not get it to turn on, so he ran.

His plans foiled, he was enraged. He went to Rigley's to decide his next move, and he found her there. He dragged her off the barstool, up the sidewalk, and into his car. He demanded to know why she was there, spending his hard-earned money, when she should be at home, preparing for a baby. She then simply lost her cool. She shouted at him—the doctors told her that day she could not conceive—when he shoved the lit cigar up into her uterus, he scarred the cervix and sperm could no longer swim through. This had to be the worst day ever for Nick. He broke her nose.

Should she have kept working, she could afford an operation to fix her faulty reproductive organs, but she was damaged goods and good for nothing.

The nicest thing he ever did for her was to smother her with the shower curtain that night, and inject way too much heroin into his veins, laying her still, cool corpse in his arms as he drifted into oblivion. Rigley found them the next day, having heard about the scene Nick created, and concerned, stopped by with a fix.

The scandal rocked the town, and the owners of the duplex sealed the back part of the house, refusing any one entry except the police, and removing themselves from the town altogether. They finally sold the home thirty years later, and this is where I come in.

The town knew the notorious abode had new owners, and they anticipated the place being opened at some point this year. They all wanted a piece of notoriety, and they did not care if it was blood on their hands or not. In fact, the bloodier the better, it seemed. Therefore, when I decided to renovate the back of the house, I was overwhelmed. Time stood still in those four rooms, and they smelled of vulgar decay. The sight of it all made me weep. I knew a bit about the failed actress's story, including the part where her murderer was her brother and her lover, and there was a fetus inside the girl's corpse, also dead, but the rest of the story had a sinister patina that was slightly indiscernible. *Why do people do the things they do?*

There was a lot of clutter in those four rooms. They were not the dirtiest tenants, but they clearly were disturbed, and disinterested in living. The girl's personal effects were hidden away in the bottom of clothing drawers, and behind boxes in closets. A stuffed bear. An empty bottle of perfume. A few photos of the boy and girl, and then, of just the girl, in black and white, beginning her modeling career. I thought about what kind of filth could destroy another human life, one so innocent and new, and I decided to sell every single item I found in that place, in an auction, and all the money would be dedicated to building a shelter for victims of domestic violence—girls and women, no matter the cost. My initial plan was to incinerate the goods, but this plan now came upon me like an epiphany, and waves of sobbing relief washed over me as I fell into a pile on the dirty bedroom carpet, confused as to why their pain was mine, as well.

The next day I found a peroxide bottle in the medicine cabinet labeled with an expiration date of June 1955. That struck me as very eerie since that was a month before the boy and girl died. There were dead flies all along the bottom of the wastebasket, and the tub was a rusty shade of crimson. The entire place would need to be gutted.

I let several friends into the place the next day, and they just started helping me without saying a word. We were all possessed by some universal mourning, sprung into action by a tragedy, working our way towards redemption. I asked myself if we were complicit in this evil world? Sometime later I got my answer.

We were opening the house to the public, labeling items for sale—remarkably high prices, and people would pay. Each of us "workers" kept a few items, feeling that we needed to maintain some sort of physical connection with the travesty of humanity we witnessed, or just a sign of perpetual mourning for a beautiful young girl. I found a few letters behind the medicine cabinet, that the girl wrote to an unidentified recipient. She did not sound like any woman I had ever known. She was so broken, and delusional, that she became science fiction. A sentient doll. A mechanized mannequin, clinging to sanity.

The worst part of the rooms was the bedroom. Once we removed the tattered linen, sour old bloodstains permeated the flaking mattress, and I swore I saw fingerprints—gripping—the mirror above the bed. Power does terrible things to a person. I wondered if we would avoid evil altogether if we all had access to unlimited resources in the universe? I felt the sadness give way to a numbing feeling coming over me, spreading through my skin like liquid nitrogen, as my friend pulled me out of the room. He assured me they would take care of it. I was as tired as a dead star.

I kept going, then, throughout the day, mobilized by the remnants of fuel left for us in these spent rooms, wanting to make sure people paid their proper respect as they entered the auction site. The last minute before we were to begin the bidding came, and I decided to just let people buy what they wanted, at the prices we fixed. They came, the people, like swarms of insects, ravishing the innards of a dead pig. It was hard to keep track of the time. I felt a renewed sadness at profiting from the tragedy of this poor girl and her insane companion, and at the vigor of people eating it up. I did not advertise my intentions; only my friends were aware of the next step, the building of the shelter. Still, they came, and a few times I had to ask people to leave, when they tried to pay me less for a soiled nightdress or a tarnished silver elephant strung on a cheap blackened necklace. A few of the local college students were creating a stir in the bathroom, laughing at something, and I screamed at them. I screamed at them to get out, and I was so vengeful they scampered like cockroaches exposed to light. They scampered like the boy would have if someone, anyone, would have come to the girl's rescue, and threatened the boy with castration. He deserved to die, she did not. That is the only certainty I have in this world.

I also kept her pictures. I hide them and try to forget I have them in an effort to diminish the overwhelming force of emotion they elicit whenever I take them out. Conversely, there are times when I am low, and I am drawn to them like a moth to a flame, like some mechanism inside of me that guides me to the sky, so that I can fly closest to the sun.

Nighttime Cavity

The bedraggled passengers did not appear cold, just bewildered. They were tired, too. The body is as fragile as it is strong. There was a man positioned by the point where my family and I disembarked from that ghostly figure of a boat, and he was explaining our predicament in record time. We would be living in the dank and monochrome subterranean tunnels until such time that we escaped. Folds in time would facilitate our escape, but we must identify them, find them, and access them, like hitting a hidden sweet spot in the dark. No problem. What the hell was he even talking about?

We were only allowed to disembark with what we could carry, and to retrieve the rest meant a long journey from where we spent our days, to where we started the sentence. According to our guide, we simply fell through a fold in time, and it was just our dumb luck. No one in particular was fated, and no one controlled the folds. They were just natural manifestations of time and space. We all looked like we stepped out of Dickens' London, although later when I first accessed the fold in time in an attempt to dislodge my family and I from the sentence, everyone looked like they were filming an episode of The Love Boat.

We carried as much food and weaponry as possible back to a sheltered area in the rocks that formed the walls of our domicile. My Mother failed to see the point in my committing to priority space makeshift spears, knives, and other assault-like improvisational material, but a few days into our unloading, a young, dark woman started intimating towards a fight. She was banging a piece of pipe around on a steel railing that lined a passage winding up the tunnel form the water, and it was hard to decipher her ranting, but I could only assume she wanted out of the sentence. Who didn't? I kept my weary eyes in a constant rotation from her to the ground beneath me and was ever so grateful when she shut up. I did not want to have to use the mallet I found in the cargo hold portion of the ship. As her instincts would tell her that I would raise it over my head and attempt to strike her head, I would surprise her by raising the mallet from beneath myself and striking her knees. I did not want to kill anyone, but I would be very clear about my intention to survive, unharmed, along with my family.

I made friends with a boy on the ship that first fell through the fold and carried us below, and he suggested we waste no time is beginning to pursue a way out. He heard rumors that folds in time only occurred only every few years, so we did not want to miss them when they happened. When our food was gone, and people started turning on each other, and dying, we would be too desperate to fortify our chances for survival. I felt strong, and we soon set out through the infinite subterranean tunnels to seek the way to the surface and hope for a transport back to our rightful place in time. Once we found the fold, we had about a day to get whomever we wanted through it, and surely, we would avoid the river for the rest of our lives.

We ascended into a sunny port, filled with people in nautical themed attire, sounds of frivolity permeating the bright horizon. The tunnels took many hours to traverse, then we climbed innumerable levels of steel stairs to get to the doorway that simply emptied us out into a tropical paradise. This was the past, still, but not too far off from our rightful time, and certainly closer than the time we seemed lodged in below. We had a mission to find the way back to our own time before we ran out of food.

We were also transformed: we looked like something out of a synthesizer fueled neon dreamscape. The place where we entered through the fold was a harbor, with luxuriously oversized boats and hats. People were making their clickety-clack way over a wooden dock that led to an enormous party filled with sun and fun. Since we weren't quite sure what the hell we were doing from the get-go, we followed along. The waves of pleasure gripped up shortly therein.

The smell of food was immeasurable; whole animals, roasted and toasted, and served next to rainbow rosaries of vegetables and delicacies of all variety. No one gave us any notice, until a young man just about our age came over and offered us champagne. He said that the secret to getting along in these soirees was to drink a lot and look exhausted by the sheer magnitude of all the fun we were all having. I immediately thought it was an odd thing to say, but that was mostly on account of me secretly wishing he knew who we were and had a way to help us. Not too soon after we were swaying to the lulling wave of heat and ocean swells and smooth jazz, he started off towards the upper deck of the looming vessel and finally, jackpot: he told us that the way out was through the way in.

My boy friend immediately turned his bewildered, terse lips into a gnarly sneer; he was not amused. I do not think it mattered at all, really, since the way we came in was as much of a mystery to us as the way back, through, out, or in between. We ate. And then we drank some more.

And we formed our plan.

A beautiful blonde in a white linen dress dove into the water, and her suitor followed suit. Soon, several other bored disciples joined the couple, and there was much merry-making in the swirling gray waters, as twilight descended upon the surface of the sound. Their squeals were enough to turn the dead pig over, and, as if he read my mind, my companion hurled the charred swine into the water with them. Some members of the crew still on board slowly moved their eyes towards us, their mouths trailing behind mirroring cool terror as if the worst they'd ever known was coming to bear. They were too stupefied to move. We, however, were not, and we hastily made our way back over the wooden bridge and disappeared into the harbor plaza. A fog was rolling in, and we were hoping to be shielded by the thick night.

Not a soul came after us, and when the cackling of drunk swingers was behind us, we sat on a curbstone to consider our fate. The fog was dampening our clothing and giving us a chill. I was on the verge of tears—the frustration seeping out of me like shit in a diaper—when I began to disappear. I brought my hands up to wipe my intruding tears and I saw the outline of pine trees through my veins. My friend was not looking at me, off in his own realm of mystification, so I put a hand on his leg, and it moved right through his knee cap. The little squeak that came from my evaporating throat was enough to bring his eyes back to mine, although those were fading, too. The green of the trees was there, in the place where his irises overlapped the forest, and we effervescently billowed out into orbits of mist.

Put Alex in the Abyss

Alex let me out her back door just before the sun beat over the horizon. That was a good move because I did not have any shades on me, and that same old anxiety came out through the side-hatch to toss me out the door, harder. Walking out her door was not unlike the automation that dictated the past twenty hours of my life where each minute bled into the next until before I knew it, I was home. There was no time to think about where I just came from or why it was incredibly inane; there was no headspace allocated for listening to the part of my intuition that met my intellect. When the minutes shade together as the scenery goes by your little black car, there is only time for reassurance that whatever you are about to admit to yourself is just insane nonsense:

There is always war in paradise;

the guards of love are dead.

Paradise will come. I will find it, or the path will be set for me. Right now, there is only confusion because I know I am not supposed to be here. *Here* is back in bed forgetting the time before; *here* is also where I am in the rooms of women who smell foul to me after a while. There are other places I should not be but I am there because it all fits together that way.

Here in bed I hear the phone ringing from the kitchen. In my concentrated automation, I forgot to shut my door, and sometimes they call. I knew better, so I must be slipping. And I am not tired enough to fall back asleep and fight the curiosity of whether my anxiety will be exacerbated today or lessened. I have no idea what time it is as I make my way to the shower, all squinty-eyed and shaky. The cold water hits my head, the freight train comes roaring through, and my brother calls my name. The phone was for me, but it is someone he knows. I roar back at him, pretend not to care who it is, and begin getting my gear together for work tonight. Even though the time is unclear, my night must be beginning again soon.

There was a moment early one afternoon, six months after I hoped to never see a girl named Alex whose back door spurned me out, where I wondered if she wondered why I held her so tight to me. She felt good. Fantastic curves, where your over-aged hands felt their years melting away. One smooth, flat surface where once there were hardened wrinkles. This thin layer of velvet, her skin, wore my mind away from me and I had to quickly distract myself. This girl was not to be persuaded, I decided.

"Why waste time?" I asked myself. I acted against my better instincts. Letting my guard down like this could not be good, but I was not so sure it was my guard. I was just doing what came naturally. Now it was time to admit that I hated being alone, but no one was ever good enough for me.

Prisoners of War

We were prisoners of war. Some madman drove a long, orange bus with gray, ripping seats of an old cow's leather. The floor was rubber, and there was a wheelchair accessible seat, but the rubber aisles were so slim and inefficient that the chair and its inhabitant would have to fold in half to fit through.

The seats were almost full, and we seemed to make no hesitation as we rolled through busy streets, time suspended. I began conversing with other passengers, and their faces were nondescript and unrecognizable. I felt their faces held fear, but complacency ruled their chairs, their thrones made of underfed bone and nubile mind matter. They wanted to scream, and ask for direction, but they kept their conversations rolling on about the nothing at all that hides everything—every kind of wanting you could find.

I think I went to high school with all of them, but I cannot say for certain.

I sat nearer the driver, and with my back towards him, I started speaking to all the passengers, in the daylight, and to the streets, passing by: we are approaching a place I can describe, would you like to hear about it?

I saw a man with a dark, hooded coat, mentally trepanning us from the space between his eyes and the pull-strings: I am not afraid of you; our segments reconstruct in every city, beginning to end.

We were approaching an immense building, constructed of copper and fine Italian marble, spanning the entirety of two city blocks. It did more than loom—it ruled and measured everything within a 10-mile radius. The church was built in the early 1900's for the Catholics who constructed the stations of the cross inside with enough vivid imagery to pale a carnivore.

Next, we saw the building arise on our right-hand side, and the eyes on the bus shifted towards the multifaceted green that the copper aged into. My sudden majestic inquiry was rhetorical: "would you all like to witness where my madness first came to fruition?"

I stumbled over the word *madness*, because it is limiting in its use, and the whole of the spectrum that is humanity takes a lifetime of words to describe insanity still. But still, I have to start somewhere, don't I? Lean this way...

....it's a big bell, and the rejoicing sound it resembles as it swings reminded me of the prison, the war, the captors, and: why was I leading this tour all of a sudden?

Across the street was an equally immense yet rather dull all-brick hospital, and here was where my Father died. Adjacent to that was a tired corner diner, an empty parking lot, the holy trinity.

The bus slowed, its momentum countering the incline at the intersection of the divine affinity I have for bringing people back home and driving them away; but this is my home, and I decided that they can never what I see. I stepped off the bus.

The madman waved to me as he folded the bus door back in, his grin so immense I feel jarred; it was out of place, but then I recognized that he was was you, even though you died one year ago today.

When Summer Was Summer

Against the backdrop of the steel mill chimneys, pouring steam towards the powder blue sky, you were a hero. A silent hero. You melted into the backgrounds of all the old photos you kept of your youth, and even the biography they composed to tell your subtle tale, disguised your identity. It seemed that no one really knew you. Although I suppose by now your wife does. The time that passed since you were that young sojourner is twenty-five years now, and that is quite a long time when you are not so young anymore.

We happened to be closer to the same age that summer than ever before, and we were also both in Grandma's basement retrieving beer and pop when we became inseparable. Remarkably, we flew under the radar, of all the judging eyes, that belonged to the meddlers who smelled their idea of sin a mile away; they detected moments that roused their envy from twice as far away. How did we do it? There were so many of them back then, and it often felt as if they had nothing better to do than adulterate any situation that posed happiness for someone other than themselves.

Especially if they did not understand the sentiment behind the situation, but how could they ever? They did not mean to be monsters, yet the result was just the same, slithering tongues and burning black eyes, poison escaping from their spiteful mouths. Misery feeds the monsters.

Our newly shared space was delightful. We began to travel everywhere together: out to eat, out to pubs, out to stores, out to the beach, out to parties. We shared a vision of the future, a philosophy for the ages, and a similar sense of humor. I might have considered you more mild-mannered, and you might have considered me a bit wild, still we understood each other, and took solace in our shared space. We would ascend from our ventures to your room upstairs through the side door that bypassed the general living areas of your parents' house. The wooden stairs let out tiny creaks as they curved towards the third-floor landing and neared the threshold—your room was the sole occupied space, positioned next to the attic. It was stocked with maple wood matching furniture and a large, puffy brown sofa that began to bear my imprint from many late-night slumbers. I liked giggling in response to our tired silliness as we drifted to sleep. I loved seeing the slice of bright summer sun come through your musty old curtains, cueing us to begin another day together. My Mother assumed I was safe; my Father was already lost to his disease, death approaching his door, unbeknownst to us.

And your parents were busy. Your brothers were busy. They were all much too busy to keep tabs on us, which is probably why we got away with living our lives with each other for the time that we did. The few years that we did, until the future came for us. One night, after a long day at the beach, we came back to your room all sandy and sundrenched, and you joined me in the shower. Those monsters would say it was sin, but we would say it was innocence—and since we were there, the monsters could go to Hell. We loved each other, inside and out. How rare is that?

Then I began sleeping in your bed with you, and we began holding hands. We walked up and down bricked streets in the neighborhoods that lined the industrial heart of the town, our blue eyes constantly crinkled at the sides from smiling and laughing. It was not until you showed me the pictures of you and your friends the summers before we came together that I began to sense our time together would be eclipsed. These pictures showed you as a man of substance—of full knowledge and appreciation of his surroundings, and full of the energy and force to do all things good in the world. You joined the military. You served your time. You exhibited wisdom and bravery in all things, inspiring others, and you rose above the monsters all around you, even the ones in your head. You were a beacon of light, years ahead of me, in so many ways. I would love to say that all of the reasons are the reasons I was drawn to you, however I believe we shared a space that was simply made just for us, and like a brain cell and a drug, we fit. Perhaps you saw something in me that was not yet there; something barely brimming the surface, waiting to reveal itself? I would like to think so. Then again, I did love your trailblazing moustache and, for you, I always wore my low-cut summer dresses. Nature is a wily thing.

I can still see you, your blonde hair shining in the sun.

Even when I think of you now, all of my belly grows warm, and my eyes become misty, and I imagine it is a bit like heroin rushing through my veins. It is the warm embrace of contentment, excitement, and relief, all wrapped around me like a chemical buzz. Just knowing you existed fills me with the bittersweet longing of a moth to a flame. Nature is a treacherous thing.

Crickets chirping, and cars cruising down the night time freeway, you went to work one summer night, leaving me in your room with a movie to watch. I had no idea they made a movie about you, yet I was not surprised either. Half-way through the story, I could barely tell they were depicting you, the small-town boy with big dreams. They made you much more charming than you were. They also made you fall in love with an equally bright and equally shy college girl, and they made you marry her. They made you leave all of us behind in your parents' house, and they made you happy. Good for them. I stayed up the entire night, tears distorting my vision, soaking your pillow, and an irrational movie now playing in my mind. The monsters found their way to get to us, evidently.

You came and consoled me, remarkably. Who would not assume you would?— being of such heroic character, but irrationality makes people crazy. You just understood our future path better than I and mourned it with me. My timing always sucked.

The last night we spent together was two years after we bumbled around with glass bottles in our hands in the cool comfort of the basement. You had pulled my father from his mangled car and waited with me for the ambulance. It was the first time I saw you cry. You said the only thing you knew with absolute certainty was that I would be ok, and then you left the country the next day. You needed to get so far away from all of us to silence the monsters that it took you 5,000 miles to find peace. And find that girl who shared in your delusions of peace like I never could. Just like that, I never saw you again.

The Long Man

Many people considered the plague as though it were the coming of the end of the world. Kissandra felt it would take a lot more than this to destroy the planet. She was ultimately correct. She spent several months holed-up in the three-story house on Dresden Street, until signs of life began to emerge from without. Slowly, neighbors began to reconstruct their daily routines, and their surroundings. The only real damage was neglect since many refused to leave their shelters for weeks on end, and then when they did go out, they did it with a swiftness that left only room for acquiring needed resources. Kissandra walked the dogs; they walked along the perimeter of the back yard, and as the tiny dogs sniffed the ground relentlessly, Kissandra surveyed the desiccated garden plants, wondering if the ground was safe to plant again?

She was making her way in when the cats ran out. The housemates were all fearful of the animals getting too far from home and being lost for good having been taken-up by some other household; therefore, the ladies chased the cats through the yard, shrieking, until Sandy caught-up with the lot and brought the tangled mass in her arms back into the house. The scene was electrified with nervous tensions and darting eyes, all ladies looking at each other, scurrying to be still once more, invoking the impression that all was still. Too late. Frederick dipped under the doorframe at the back of the house and stepped onto the driveway with consternation. Kissandra was still standing by the garden, and he snarled at her as he glanced her way. She was not afraid of him because he never bothered with her. Truth be known, he never bothered with any of the ladies except Sandy, who was his wife. Had he missed her on his way out? What was he looking for?

The early-afternoon light was tinged with a silver haze of a winter's exit, and a few neighbors were tending their lawns. Other people were at the corner of the street reconstructing the corner store. It appeared that the sickness had run its course, and it was amazing to Kissandra that Frederick did not join in to help. He was one of the tallest men left on the planet, and he was strong. Most of the men on the planet were killed by the sickness, leaving women to pick up the pieces, and the men who did remain worked just as ceaselessly. All of the men except Frederick, that is, who did little except frighten the ladies in the house and reprimand his wife.

Frederick was so tall that when he picked Sandy up by his right hand, she came several inches off the ground, her toes dangling towards the asphalt. He demanded to know why the cats escaped? Sandy did not offer any explanation, and there would be hell to pay for her perceived insolence. The sour air escaped Frederick's elongated nostrils, warming Sandy's cheeks with the stench of cooking death. He shook her until all her hairpins fell to the black ground, and her brain bruised itself on the sides of her skull. He skulked away towards the woods across the road, and the ladies and I dragged Sandy to her bed. There she lay for an entire day until she came back to consciousness. During the night, he certainly tormented her.

Frederick was not always tall and strong and mean. Sandy married him the year before the plague, and he was just average then: average height, even temperament, moderate ambitions. During the course of their confinement in the big red house, Frederick became ill and disoriented—and eventually transformed. There was now no telling what would bring about his fits of rage. Even if all five of the ladies (including Sandy) and the two dogs and three cats tried to mutiny, he would smite them all, certainly. The beginning of his transformation manifested in his physical mutations, and once the ladies conquered their shock and horror, they decided that the silver lining was evident: Frederick would be their protector. He could also help rebuild at a much quicker rate than an average man. Not long after the brute strength appeared, did the rage follow, and Sandy was often black and blue. She was his everything. When the ladies finally decided he had to go, they were stymied: there was no way to heave him out other than murder, and none of them entertained that notion at the time.

Kissandra felt the time had come. Frederick was useless. He spent most of his time in the woods doing who the hell knows what, only returning to torment his wife. He was never satisfied. He only spoke to the rest of us ladies if he needed something and Sandy was not around. Sandy said that he asked her to remind all of us that he was the master of the house should there be any dissention.

The ladies looked for a cure the first few months after the plague disappeared and found none. There were no other cases of elongation in any of the creatures on the planet, and which one of them was going to invite doctors and scientists to mess with Frederick? Surely, Sandy would be one step closer to the grave if that were to happen. Despite his incorrigible attitude, it was clear that Frederick was fine with his existence. Sandy had long since given up the hope of seeing him restored to his former state, being relegated to a desperate state of wishing the nightmare would end, however dreadful the ending might be. The other ladies, equally, did not wish to see her dead.

The realization of the immediate implications of the extraordinary circumstances they found themselves in struck Kissandra with full force the next gloomy afternoon when Sandy finally woke from her concussion, and the animals were restless to roam. Should there be any chance at having a normal life again, Frederick would have to go. If he was not going to mend fences and replant gardens, and bring food to the table, rather simply exist to torture them all, he had to go. And where there is a will, there is a way.

The house next to the entrance of the small forest began selling fabric. The ladies owned a fully-operational dry-cleaning store. There they began to vend their tapestries, their curtains, and blankets, and they advertised their wares on the front lawn. Many people were in need of these items, having disposed of their fabrics out of fear that the plague was a bacterium that could not be washed out of their homes. Most washing machines were out of service, as well, having been overused by the desperate residents of the planet that now housed three times as many women as men. Kissandra noticed their washer broke the day Sandy was doing laundry, last summer, on a hot and humid evening. Frederick blamed Sandy, of course, and hung her on the clothesline for a day, as punishment. The rest of the ladies hid in the attic that week, out of disgust, shame, and extreme despair. Sandy never blamed them.

The evening of the gloomy afternoon found Kissandra dreaming of a riot: an uprising of all the women from miles around, overcoming Frederick with their spatulas and garden hoes, tearing him down to his knees. She sat up in the morning, sweating, holding her head in her hands. The people of the neighborhood, let alone the town, did not know of

Frederick's cruelty. Kissandra felt that the time was now for the truth to be an agent in Frederick's demise.

She cautiously made her way across the street to the ladies who sold fabrics. She began to speak with them about their wares. She proceeded to tell them more when they invited her in for tea, and they all felt quite at ease with one another. The defenses constructed by the fate of the past year melted away like the sugar cubes in the warm April afternoon. The sun was strong that day; the gloom melted away, in an encouraging coincidence—the kind that is required to inspire bravery and force. The ladies who sold fabrics helped Kissandra plan to take Frederick down for good.

Kissandra would work for the merchant ladies, selling the linens on the front lawn weekday afternoons. The only currency left in the world was coin, therefore Kissandra would deposit the coin in the till—and in the showcase tapestries used for display, in small slits along the seams. The tapestries would grow very heavy, obviously, since some were many feet tall and wide. Frederick kept an eye on the ladies selling fabrics, and Kissandra taking coin. She knew he was looking to see if Kissandra brought any coin home—which she did not, only food as pay. He also considered the interactions in terms of mutiny: was Kissandra telling the household secrets to the ladies of the land? Kissandra knew this because he made sure to remind Sandy to remind Kissandra that this would be unacceptable, by cutting Sandy's long blonde hair one night within centimeters of her head. Kissandra informed all the ladies except Sandy of her plan, updating them each afternoon Frederick went into the woods.

There was no ammunition left on the planet. Sure, there were weapons such as knives and bats and axes, but no guns of any sort. The ladies surely could have cut Frederick's throat in the night, except his hearing was amplified along with his elongation. The tapestries seemed right. Kissandra began to tell all the women who bought fabric about Frederick, and the word spread like wildfire. Not a one of them failed to appreciate the need to destroy the mutant of a man haunting the forests, eating any livestock within sight. The ladies of Kawana Grove knew that any discussion of Frederick outside the tapestry circle would result in Sandy's demise, and absolutely none of them wanted that.

Come the day of execution, the women began to pile onto the fabric-sellers' lawn. Kissandra shouted incomprehensible words across the growing crowd, as Frederick emerged from the house and made his way to the forest. She chose words that would trigger his paranoia and incite his curiosity. Sure enough, he began to dislike what he heard, and he stopped by the fabric stand in the front lawn.

The women gathered there on the lawn were not just women, but men, too, disguised as women. They had great courage that day as they began to strike Frederick with fabric lined with coin. They heaved great blows upon him, two-by-tow, three-by-three, and one-by-one. The greatest feat of all was bringing Frederick to his knees and covering him with the largest tapestry ever woven, its edges lined with coin so heavy that Frederick could not lift it off himself. He fell the ground and never rose again. The beatings continued until his last breath sucked the fabric into his mouth and kept it there. They dragged his corpse into the woods and burned the entire lot of it down. Sandy grew her hair back.

Killers

During the war to end all wars, Kyra was sold into slavery. Her husband sold her to the local magistrate who paid quite a fee for the buxom young lady. The husband left for the front, and never returned. Kyra assumed she was indentured for a life of hard labor, never realizing that she was much more valuable than that. Soldiers were dying too quickly from new diseases they were never exposed to before; the magistrate felt his great contribution to the world would be his breakthrough in finding the remedy to the most virulent strain.

Kyra was made obese. So obese she was made to lie in a bathtub for a year, while the lab doctors pricked her skin, gave her lesions, and dehydrated her to the brink. They made every attempt to break the codes—the natural encryptions that made nature tick. Kyra was burned, flayed, drowned, and made unconscious. This was the time of the living hell.

When the war was won, Kyra was released. She was a shadow of a woman. And everyone she once knew, both friend and foe, was dead. She attempted to make herself invisible. She had some gold from the magistrate's tomb. She wandered towards the western sea, to the places that looked like ancient ghost towns, and then past them to the oases.

She found a plot of land in a quaint village that had a jump on being rebuilt. It was small—enough for a small house and a tiny bit of land. Although no one had the fuel to drive, Kyra bought a small camper and parked it in her yard. She didn't have the gold too build a house, so the camper would have to do for now.

Her presence did not go unnoticed by the neighbors. At first, they resented her ownership of fuel. When they realized she only purchased enough to park the camper, they assumed she was an interloper. She was, after all, swarthy, and covered in scars. She was still beautiful, but she looked like an outlander. The neighbors gossiped about how she came to be in their midst, and why she wasn't lodging with her own kind. However, they soon paid her little notice as she kept to herself and was very, very quiet. They only saw her at night, seated beside her small campfire, built behind a screen. She was a shadow—almost invisible—and they soon forgot about her for the most part.

Kyra eventually shed her rags for more intact clothing. She met a local barkeep who fell in love with her; she cooked for his restaurant and he paid her handsomely. They eventually afforded a two-story house: white, with black shutters, in the ancient federalist design that was re-popularized after the war to end all wars. Square boxes were simple, and safe.

She had a child with the barkeep. She eventually died in the white house, and the child, grown up, had her own child. They always kept to themselves. When the grandmother's book recalling the terrible events of her life within the living hell was published, none of the neighbors knew it was the odd family in the small white house in the middle of the block. It was each subsequent generation of women born into the white house that carried the weight of knowing their shared heritage. This meant, they could hardly ever look anyone directly in the eye. Fear, shame, sorrow, and malice comprised their shared DNA.

But when the grandchild became a woman, she became prescient. She saw the future of the world, re-inventing itself, and re-populating itself with alien humanlike creatures. She saw history turning itself over and over again. Within these visions, she found peace. She married a schoolteacher, and gave birth to a son, just before the schoolteacher died.

The son was a scandalous boy. He had the sight, too, but he chose to ignore it. He hated the legacy his great-grandmother left them to contend with since the book was constantly being republished—like a legend. Even though no one connected him with the family, he was angry that he could not protect his loved ones from the killers before them.

He was swarthy and charming. His mother wanted him to enjoy his life and leave a better legacy for those to come. But he did not take this seriously. He frequented the bars and got up for work every morning. He let his mother think he was an unfaithful soul who could not love a woman. The truth was, he was just afraid of the photos in the attic. He was afraid of the shadows by the campfire. He was afraid of what men did to women. Even though he loved them all.

His mother had a yard sale, and she met a pale, vibrant woman who purchased some old books from the bin in the driveway. They were related to the living hell, and when his mother revealed that she was a descendant of Kyra Dragdonovit, the young woman was immediately enamored.

Pyle's mother and the young woman sat in the yard the remainder of the day, comparing notes. Pyle's mother had the original copy of Kyra's book, and it held information that the published editions did not. The young woman was in awe of how Pyle's mother saw the world in the aftermath of the war to end all wars, and the living hell, and the two women felt kindred to one another.

The two women spent much time together over the next few months. They exchanged light and dark, like the colors of their skins. Pyle saw the young woman and wanted her. Of course, his mother had already warned the young woman against the charms of her young son. She could not take him seriously. This meant a great deal to the old woman. The young woman could sense this but felt there was no threat looming in the guise of this man and his desires. The young woman was unaware of Pyle's attraction.

One exceedingly sunny day, he invited the young woman to a party. Pyle's mother was out of town, and he said that there was a party in a room over the old drive-in theater. The young woman found herself wanting to go despite not wanting to be near Pyle. He suddenly felt threatening. He suddenly, too, appeared handsome and desirous. That's how these things happen.

When the young woman arrived, Pyle was waiting. When she wondered aloud if anyone else due to attend the party but Pyle, she knew he had lied. She began to visibly tremble as he took her hand and drew her into further into the room. She feared his vengeance. She did not know that he felt her trembling as a sign of her desire. She felt the guilt of generations as she pressed her lips to his. She knew their love would be the ultimate betrayal for Pyle's mother.

But why was love so cruel? Why should the young woman and her new paramour be punished for their feelings—these things that cannot be controlled? Feelings of guilt and self-loathing—hate and misunderstanding—drove the world to extinction.

The Psychic

The little girl was me, and it is only recently that I came to this realization. She was ten years old when we first met, and she was dressed for the deceptive chill of early spring days. She insisted that the cause of my Father's disappearance could be found in my grandparents' back yard, back by the miniature golf course. This information had me quite nonplussed; where to begin in dissecting this mystery? Immediately I pictured the focused acumen of cadaver dogs, sniffing through the damp spring grasses, searching for a buried body. Perhaps he was in the adjacent garden—my Father, feeding the pea pods and the strawberries, the watermelons and the baby tomatoes? That was mildly acceptable—death feeding life, of course, yet it still stung like a red-hot branding iron to the heart, to think I might never see him again. What did this little girl know?

She followed the golf course from my grandparents' back yard into the neighbor's yards, down a house or two, until she came upon a row of hedges. She paused there and pointed at the length of them, as they began at one corner of the house, and stretched to the other, her tiny porcelain hand moving over the face of the dew-strung air with confidence. The obvious explanation for her insinuation was that my Father was buried there; upon closer examination one could see, however, that the hedges were there for nearly twenty-years. My Father only disappeared a few days ago, thereby rendering this deduction completely useless. The little girl began to move closer to the hedges when some neighborhood gentlemen came to play through the course, and they found her, and questioned her for hiding from them.

"What are you doing there? Are you supposed to be out here in this chill?"

She ran, quite vigorously, from the hedges to the street, fading into the twilight dusk with leaves trailing her wake and a few new scratches on her chilled little hands. The old men played through.

The next morning, I followed her to the wrong side of town. The trailers began behind the double hills, a few blocks from my grandparents lower-middle-class neighborhood filled with identical houses, paneled and squared, with neat yards and concrete driveways. The dirt-poor neighborhood behind the hills changed the landscape from a green cornucopia of sedated bliss to a dust bowl of impoverished orange haze. I had never been here before, but the little girl seemed to know where she was going and came upon a row of trailers with purpose. The structures started out white, and then time turned them the color of newborn rust. In an alley behind two rows of them stood a row of utility lockers, the same color, the same age. The little girl just walked over the street-trash, gravel surfaces, and decayed vegetation, straight towards the locker on the end. It was unlocked, and she fished her little hand right into it, rummaging around with purpose. What did this little girl know so well?

She extracted a locked box from the locker and picked the lock with a nail file. Is this believable? The lockers were neglected, and the metal surfaces in and around them weakened the strength of the atomic tension holding everything together. Residents were moving out of the neighborhood, into new projects across town. They began to forget about the missing girl, her cupid face and blonde curls fading from their memories. The missing girl's mother spent her days weeping, and the neighbors were sympathetic. They were also enraged that the killer was not found. They knew that the adorable four-year old putti-faced baby girl must be dead, since she went missing over a year ago, and most missing children cases resulted in homicide. Child killers. They were the worst. The neighborhood would love to lynch, and they would love to lynch the residents over the hills since they had seemingly little sympathy for the missing girl's plight. The police exerted such minimal effort on the case, it was laughable. Without the means to fight back, the people in the trailers just stewed.

I was not aware that a little girl was missing, until the little girl with the nail file and purpose introduced me to the evidence. The box held a half-dozen warped Polaroid photos depicting the cupid-faced girl with arms entwined with an equally sweet looking little boy. This hardly seemed suspicious until I saw the reflection in the window, of the man taking the picture, the last pictures taken before the child disappeared.

He looked *very* familiar to me.

Vision Thing

The college town could be a cruel town, but I ignored the sinister undertones connected with the past—pervading the present long into the future—and carried about my business. The night the vandals came to the school, I wasn't even supposed to be there (of course). I really don't know who they were, but there was no distinct ancestry to them and all I can remember is the noise…and the violence. They shot Mina right in front of me and I felt she deserved it in some horrific way (—don't worry, she lived), and that this was all just a part of nature, which I wanted to stay on the other side of. I didn't pray, I just hoped that it wasn't my time. I wanted to live past this and move on. I also wanted the vandals brought to justice.

Maybe they were a rebel force—I still don't know. I don't know what they wanted or how they got there, or even how they were captured, but thankfully they were, and I survived. Their weaponry didn't seem all that sophisticated, but it certainly got the point across, and as I was shoved through the hallways filled with chaos, they dispensed of me in an old farmhouse, some acres across campus. In the paleness of the moonlight, I still saw blood and anguished faces. I suffered some bruises and felt all my remaining energy leave me as I passed out on a cold, dirt floor.

When I woke, I was being carried through the farmhouse, lit with a hundred light bulbs and full of musty odors. I heard the wailing of sirens and frantic chatter of hundreds of people; I was eventually placed on a gurney underneath some oak trees. I could pick out specks of light moving across the night sky, my eyes moving with the slowness of time-lapsed photography, as if a perverted form of Braille was being laid out before me to see. Then silence came. I was never able to remember any more than that, and although I felt terrible about not being able to help the authorities with any details as to motives or even sequences, I moved on from that night in a curious way.

I never had any dreams about the night. I never suffered any trauma. I was never scared for unapparent reasons, night or day, and felt that my immediate relocation must have saved me from being forever attached to that tragic evening.

Then last night I finally had a dream—or a nightmare, if you will, and it felt the ending of the beginning…it felt like the rest of the story that I had tried so hard not to see. There were two lovers involved, one black and one white, and all of their blood was spilling out.

The first part of this new dimension placed me in the entranceway of the farmhouse—a large vestibule, with barrels full of goods ready to sell—not to local consumers, but to tourists. Everything was shiny and new. I was in the place as it looked before the fire, and I fondled the tourist information pamphlets as I walked along the periphery, before bumping into Harold. Harold had a shiny white head and wore beige plaid suspenders atop his white pressed shirt, yet beneath his wire rim glasses, his eyes were that of a boy. His presence confused me at first until he reassured me that he was there to help, and that's when he stopped the world.

He asked me what I wanted most in this farmhouse and I thought for a minute or so, surveying the now crowded vestibule filled with noisy adults and obnoxious children, cringing should they run into some fixture. *No respect*, I thought. And so, I answered Harold: I wanted the noise to stop.

And it did. Everything did. Everyone and everything froze in its place, except the weather, for I could still hear the rooster compass swinging around on its rusty hinge above us. In fact, it was the FIRST time I heard it, and I think I almost wet myself between a mixture of fear and excitement. My body squeezed itself together and slowly took up the guts to look towards Harold, and there he was, ten feet away and smiling at me. He was moving and so was I. My first steps between the frozen bodies were towards him, escalating my voice to normalcy in an effort to find out what the hell was going on. He smiled at me, and waved me towards him, saying something about finally getting what I wished for, and it was always there for me I just couldn't see it, etc. Nonsense yet it made sense because I was in it so how could it not? As he made his way into a dark, wood-planked corridor, I was tempted to knock a dirty 7-year old over off his axis.

The inside of farmhouse was a hundred times more beautiful than the outside because it had a shine about it. The blue and brown paint must have been the glossy type, and the surreal nature of such old floors and ceilings polished to look new gave it all a tinge of disingenuous glamour. I felt I should be afraid. Harold kept me too busy to feel anything but trepid excitement as we walked past the kitchen, listening to our breathing and the creaking of the wood floors. Harold began talking as we entered the sitting room, and he instructed me to take a seat.

"This land has a lot of history that nobody knows about. We're only going to see part of it tonight, and I can see that you are brave, so stay that way—as you have nothing to fear, of course, but do stay out of the way. Do follow my instructions. All the answers will come." He was smiling reassuringly throughout his entire monologue.

"You are the first one I have taken in, you know? And I can tell already that you trust me. I trust you, too. Doesn't it feel good to be walking here even though we know that such terror and tragedy is here alongside the happiness?" He was trailing off now, as his smile faded, and he transformed into someone less awake and alive, and I wondered if this was my chance to ask him about the "what the hell was going?" part of my reaction—but he beat me to it:

"I am a little tired, that's all, but it's no matter. And I'd offer you a whisky, but the house is dry since ghosts don't drink, it seems. No—they aren't really, ghosts, but they aren't really alive either so…I hope you have come to the conclusion by now that I can only tell you what I have. I'm not a riddle man, just a middle man, and I certainly like you." He perked back up and slapped his lap with both hands as if to signal our time to move it. I stood up with him and pressed my skirt down as if to signal back. *Weird.*

I was befuddled. And I thought that to myself, too, and then sort of giggled to myself because that's a funny word, and Harold resisted for a few seconds then asked…he said that was a new one by him! I suddenly started to feel like we had that whisky after all. Until we started up the main staircase, a definitively sobering experience as the wood creaking echoed back to us from the silence and the darkness looming from above like death. Harold grabbed my hand. If I wasn't so scared and befuddled, I would have a better narrative for you at this time. I would like to know why I was captivated by this odd character and trusted him immediately despite the unknown distance between us; years, months, miles, meters, who knew? All I could do was look and peer and search until a light came on and Harold shuffled me into a closet in the first room—a sewing room, of sorts.

This is when Gibby entered. All the lights of the house came on now, and I saw this towering black man dressed in denim overalls and full of concern, leaping up the stairs. Angeline met him outside the sewing room door, and Harold and I could see everything since we were in the closet, but the door wasn't completely shut.

Gibby and Angeline were presently in collusion regarding the matter of what to do with me, insisting they doubted they could share. At first I thought they were arguing about who would tell me their side of a story first, and perhaps I would be asked to sit in judgment or bring their story to the living; none of this was accurate. They both stopped mid-argument to stare at me through the slit in of the closet door, and this is what their eyes said:

We're not alive and we're not dead. What those men did here will be addressed, and you needn't be concerned with that. You need to fall in love with one of us, so that we can be free. In return, you will be free, freer than you've ever known yourself or anyone else to be. Your heart will decide. And by heart, we mean everything that has led us to you. Just let everything else go. Everything that has distracted you from the core of you, and all the injustice you think you know, doesn't matter now. Those lost 'souls' are miserable without you.

I searched their faces to see their lips moving and their chests to see their hearts beating, but time began to speed up and before I was aware of the next moment, Gibby was leading me down the stairs, asking me if I danced, the colors our world slowly bleeding out of frame.

Soliloquy

I knew what my daughter was thinking. I knew that she was angry with me. If only I had been true to myself and kept moving towards the unknown, life would have worked itself out. Now I find that everything is out of my hands, but that which I always sought to know. Instead, the answers, the questions, are rushing through me. I am afraid I have always been afraid, and that fear has brought me to this moment in time. My daughter's thoughts are the comfort I have been seeking.

She looked well some time ago, my daughter. She looked beautiful and I had to concentrate on all of her words because my senses were assaulting me in ways I never knew a man might experience. Her smell wafted in as aching familiarity. It was all too tangible, for I could touch myself and stir but a layer of skin to evoke the same essence. Nothing of her face was lost in my mind, but I found I had to break down and let the strength of her presence in. Why, just by bearing alone she could dismantle the staunch opinions of every family member here in the room with me. They must have seen her power long ago thereby their treatment of her was defensive and lackluster. They were the faucets of my youth, the declination of our souls—hot, cold; hot, cold…drip, drip, LEAK.

I believe that I began to leak before Jade walked out. I remember phoning my daughter and blathering on about one thing or another when the subject of my rifle under my bed slipped in and out. I had no intention of telling anyone anything, yet her untenable persuasion coerced me by surprise. The power to end the confusion and heartache was something the alcohol helped me to harness. The alcohol was of use (other than as an anesthetic), and I must have known it all along. That's why I kept drinking—it enabled me. When my daughter's mother left me some time ago, I did not care.

"I am a loner," I declared, and that is still very true.

No one can understand me and damn those who keep trying with their incessant and ignorant attempts. Jade had been close to me like the sand to the sea, and she was the one I would have let be my ocean; I would have let her in. Unfortunately, she was with me out of desperation and indebtedness. I saved her from herself, and she loved me for that. She was my last saving grace, and I loved her for that. Her cavernous brown eyes hypnotized me and became immortalized in my mind. When we made love, her long, dark hair swept over my face like relief from a hot desert soak. Her pale face held a quietness that was reflected in her voice, and in the words that she would allow to escape. In time, I knew she would open up to me. At least, I thought she would.

When we had the baby, it was all supposed to change. Even though I was ten years her senior, I was still a good-looking dude that could shake like the rest of them. I could have two, three, even four more children with her and still not be old. I would have done that for us. We should have married a long time ago and then had Seth, but he was born just the same. That was a bond I knew Jade always wanted. My daughter was just a little girl when Jade first rejected her, but I finally understand that such power packed into her little form must have shown through. My daughter was my true kindred love with a chance at getting through to me, and this aroused great jealousy in my Jade. Isn't that something—how others could recognize it, deny it, be so affected by it, and I could not? Seth would be a bond that Jade and I created, and our love could only grow from there.

He wasn't even two years old when she took him from me. Most definitely, burned my soul and dumped it all out across the world like death's ashes. I could not put it all back together again. I had acquiesced to her requests that I quit drinking and cut down on the smoking, but I would be damned if everyone else in the world could do it and I couldn't. I would be damned.

She was beginning to break down Jade's denial, my daughter. A long time ago, her young picture was framed on my dresser and Jade hated to see it. She smashed that picture to the ground, and spit on it.

I thought, "What could my little daughter do to invoke such hatred in a grown woman?" Actually, she had not done anything at all. She was just breaking down the visiting demons. Should I admit that Jade had mental problems? Must have. We would lie in bed at night, I can envision it now quite clearly: the summer breeze was billowing the window sheers as they half-heartedly reflected the moonlight. Our sheets are cool, and her skin is porcelain. I turn to her as she nestled just below my chin, and ask her why she doesn't like my daughter? She replies with only a soft moan of defensiveness; indeed, it was more of an answer than that question had ever received before. I believe I may never hear the words for it from her now because I have a feeling I will not see Jade again.

These thoughts evoke a fearful agony that washes away the pain I am feeling as I lie in this antiseptic chamber. One thought of even the most remotely related, miniscule instance of life reminds me of Jade to the point of no control. I am marooned in that sea of sorrow, and she won't even be my sea! I never doubted that she was the one with the problem. I may have had a few vices, but I was a good person and a good provider, and I loved her. She is a stinging torrential downpour. She hurts more than the needle pricking my skin, depositing ink. I remember wanting to carve out the parts of me that wanted my family to accept me, even though I was a loner. A loner deserves recognition and respect. A loner seeks love, but can never truly make it his own, for that is the antithesis of being a loner.

I talked to Jade some time ago. She refused to see me or let me see Seth because she claimed I was too heavy; that I weighed her down when she saw me. Sure, with guilt and love, and all of the feelings she was denying for whatever insane reason her mind told her to do so. She said that I was not ready to be all that I should be, and that Seth needed a better man. I knew then that Seth might not be mine. I always suspected there was a part of her that would not be tamed, and that would lead her to another man to satisfy her insanity. I was the best she ever had, and it was not my fault she wouldn't talk to me. Tell me my downfalls, and due change will happen. We are not all perfect and she should have come to me! I just couldn't move forward with the suspicion that he is not mine and, that she never was. I can't be bothered with that. I just want everything the way it was.

Sans the alcohol, maybe.

So many were in the shadows surrounding me before, I am sure, but my daughter cleared the room. As she moves close to me, I feel her taking my hand in hers. Her skin is pale and young like Jade's once was, and her eyes are full of my sea of sorrow. She is crazed with the fever of life and her growing disenchantment with all that once was is evident. Her hopes for what she will become are leaking out. After she sorts it through, she will probably admit and accept that she is a loner, as I am.

My daughter leans over to my ear and whispers as she weeps, "I know what you're thinking, Daddy. You're thinking that you love me so much, but you have disappointed me. That's just not true. I know how much you love me, and I love you, too. You are greater than time allowed. All of this grief— I will own it now.

"I do know what you're thinking..."

This Time Around

This time around the setting is the same, but the peculiarity lies within the cast of characters: wrong side of the family and wrong dead Aunt; I usually see the Huns.

I submit very little abnormality to it being a Thanksgiving beside a neighboring millionaire's pool out behind my Grandmother's house. All is liquid cool and sublimating for a hidden winter sun. I took to diving right into the deep-end of the fairly extensive oasis, fully clothed. The gathering of people was still indoors, keeping me a safe distance from my requirements, to decide whether or not to eat or what kind of drink to make, or even worse, to engage in cursed banal conversation. I celebrated my illusion of liberation, bobbing and weaving, as the oversized tee shirt heavily clung to me.

I recognized a stranger as my half-hearted stealth floated me over to the shallow-end of the pool. One of my cousins marched outside via the patio doors and introduced me to the curly haired brunette, at which time I immediately forget both their names. The stranger stood poolside, then dove in, parting curls in the lagoon, and I quickly swam away from him. It just wasn't time yet. I pushed myself out.

Back inside the house, I am in my dearly deceased Aunt Tilde's room, and all is seductively silent. I think my cousins keep Auntie's things around to keep her memory around even though she died an old enough age to deserve to not be made a mockery of by their neurotically infested motivations. She collected an array of costume jewelry featuring beetles, now commonly referred to as scarabs as if all were suddenly Egyptian and enlightened. Aunt Tilda was not that ancient, was not that wise, was more innocent than we are, and her beetles were a fashion trend. I finger a gold and red enamel bug, the size of a half-dollar, letting the sun reflect off a grotesquely costumed head. With a sharp glinting of sunlight in my eye, I look into the mirror, half-blind. What secrets I would love to uncover, just to know that there was an underworld to all this reality, in between what we see and what we imagine, pacifying some lunacy.

I felt flushed with bullion and heat in an ancient tomb. In a way, the silence wrapped around me like a sleeper hold and little, long-bearded men with high glittering hats came though the room to light a tube and pass smoke over me. A tide of heat-quaking mass expanded through layers of air, and Auntie's bed felt welcoming as I stretched out to seek oblivion.

Later in the evening, the poolside stranger sits with me in the living room while I sip on a refreshment, and we begin to giggle. I think the time I spent in that fairly haunted room, made me lament the unknown full on—like a helium gas expanding in my mind. Everything was breathing with heaving gestures and full-blown expulsions of breath; sweat beaded on my brow and the stimulation caused such restlessness, everything was rendered primal. I wanted to strike-out, but I'd been burned before, so I smothered the flame for the sake of conformity and tried to laugh appropriately.

The stranger was tall, thin, pale, and kind. Borne of his casual demeanor, my assumption was that he didn't much care for me (but I never think they do). I was fine with pleasantries and getting on with someone who did not know not to talk about what others never talked about. At first I didn't care where he came from, and then after he left, I did. I believe that is rather normal, and I ascribe the mark of human tragedy to it, that which none of us living within the half-cognizant layers of the cosmos can escape, although it is all slightly more endurable than a war. Of course, I never saw the stranger again, and I am pretty sure he was the one.

The Summer Circled Back Around to Us

The summer circled back around to us with electricity. At the age of fourteen, who was I to know that the currents running through my bones were meant to be grounded, channeled into a world so much larger than my life currently afforded? That I could be a part of this life held a certain enticement but that I could control my life electrified me. Everyone around me seemed without will, and there is no way for a child to combat that morose foreboding unless they are truly gifted—or so a good friend once told me. Too many disbelievers and non-seers shaped my formidable years. My mind was set to break free from their onslaught. A crusade, if you will, to prove themselves right.

The summer up north is inescapably alive. Sunshine everywhere, so bright you cannot hide, cannot save your skin or shield your eyes, and people seem to rise along with the burning intensity. The noise from the sunlight, the noise from the people, is enough to drive one back indoors and scatter the synchronicity. Solace is found under weeping willow trees, the breeze transferring its energy: from tree to you, from you to the sky, hide your eyes, daydream everyone else away. Then, to go to the beach, swim far out, until your feet don't touch the ground, and all the screaming children, like lobsters boiling in a rabid sea, fade away.

To escape the clutches of a mundane summer, and to find the source, the electricity of this particular summer, I assented to a two-week vacation with my family. We drove along the lake, through sleepy towns and heat-warped intersections, an hour or so, to the camp site. I longed for the empty sea, the lonely plains, the weeping willows, the seductive faces of intrigue, but found instead, log cabins, small yards, cliffs barring our way to the sea, and a playground. If I ever spent a moment on an industrial playground while seeking recluse in the great outdoors, surely that was my demise. But no, I never did. Essentially, I wanted to disintegrate into the earth and resurface somewhere else.

I also wanted to run rampant with restlessness and carelessness—freedom from school, chores, curfews, air conditioners, bad television. In the deep night of the woods, anything was possible, wasn't it? We built fires, my father and I, and perfection seeped into his teepee of wood, facilitating the proper air flow to run those flames up to the stratosphere and back. He drank beer in those days so his breath was tinged with fermentation. His laughter was the nicest sound I ever heard. In my awkward state of existence, acceptance from him, from anyone, was electricity to my soul, and I never stopped building fires.

As the first few days passed, filled with sunshine, brewing with anticipation, I fell into a routine that I solemnly enjoyed. With mouth gaping horror I discovered that my cousin had indeed brought along a television along so as to not miss her soap operas. I tried not to be in the cabin during those scheduled viewings. I would read one of the several novels I savored while sunbathing. Just a football field away was the public showers. I trekked up each day to bathe, only to dirty myself much later, of course. Eventually, I spurned my aunts' admonishment and took my showers at night the way I always did at home. Around the third day at camp, we discovered a trail across the small dirt road leading to our cabin, and next to the only cabin adjacent to us, which led down through the cliffs and out to the sea. The public access to the beach was actually quite a drive up the small dirt roads, and we were all loath to get in the car just to access our lake. I would take this newly-discovered trail several times a day.

After passing by the adjacent cabin by the cliff once, twice, then the third time yielded sounds of inhabitants. Later in the evening, I looked across our site, some 50 yards to the cliffside, and identified the inhabitants: four young men with long flowing hair. From that moment on, my eyes were often drawn to that cabin, drawn to the electricity that was generated by the wonderful cavorting of campers in the wild. More specifically, drawn to the shadow of an unidentified, shared consciousness.

Our camping staples were with Kool-Aid, soap operas, bug spray, country music and church on Sunday. If all of these weren't enough to drive me mad, I was chided for preferring my meat cooked medium-rare. What camping expedition did not allow for pink meat? Furthermore, what blasphemy existed in worshipping God in the GREAT OUTDOORS? Obviously, this beyond my youthful comprehension.

But let us examine the grass that I laid upon while reading countless novels. Mother Nature's grass, God's straw, my bed, so soft and fragrant with stale morning dew, clover nectar, and residual summer rain. I was never afraid to walk barefoot; I never bothered to get a blanket. Regardless of who made it, I was grateful as I lay there.

Upon this grass I lay the first day of the last week of our sojourn. It was a Saturday morning, sun out early, laundry hanging from a clothing line, mix tapes made of radio favorites sat next to me for easy accessibility—when the mood shifted, so then my music needed to follow. My aunts and their favorite girl-child, Laurel, were headed out to a craft show in the nearest town (near the church, I assumed) and I had zero, let me repeat dear aunties, ZERO interest in spending my precious time looking at twisted yarn. Fortunately, my Father had arrived the night before and I was also looking forward to hanging out with him. He would play his boombox much louder once they left. *So, go, go without me, you will not miss me, I know!* Yet it was not my presence, it was their control that was at stake here.

My Father was busy unpacking his truck and setting up his campsite near the firepit, engaged in wilderness-type preparations as my female companions were dressing, as I was adjusting my turquoise bikini (my first, *take a bow*). I thought the entire world would now suspend itself and I would take control. However, the electricity shifted its allegiance to my Aunt who was ever so dismayed when I told her that I was not going to the craft show with them.

"Why aren't you dressed? Aren't you coming?" She asked with a slightly high-strung nasal whine.

"No. I am going to stay here with Dad." I was surprised that it was an issue.

"Well, I don't see what for. There's nothing to do here!" She raised her voice to me and I was wondering if anyone else was witnessing this mounting, unwarranted attack. She looked at me from the porch, through her wire rimmed glasses, too big for her head, and her curls bounced with emphasis. My blue eyes already began to well with tears, *I am so weak*, I thought.

"I am going to read my book and lay in the sun." My voice started to crack and I prayed to my grass and the sea and her God that she could not tell I was intimidated. But she could, and it doesn't matter, so she blew harder. It was as though the whole world was her audience, when in truth, it is just her, my Father, and me outside the small cabin.

"Ah, the only reason she wants to stay here is those boys."
She pointed across the small dirt road and I swear I could
have keeled over with embarrassment and injury.

Instead, I stood with my mouth hung open, straddling my
lounge chair. My father was equally shocked and countered in
my defense, asking what was wrong with her and completely
refuting her claim. The real question was: what did she care
anyway?

They were yelling at this point, but I couldn't hear them
anymore. I was already close to the public restrooms. Crying
in the urinal, I heard my sobs echo and I feel like a complete
criminal. Worst of all, I felt nothing but vengeful towards my
Aunt. She always was an evil bitch. She was making me one,
too.

I did not return to the site until I was sure they were gone.
She never apologized (she never did) and my Father only
plead that he did not know what her problem was. But more
disturbing than not understanding her perceived hatred, her
malice, was knowing she was partly right. I did prefer to
linger, to absorb that energy that seemed ripe for the picking.

Whatever she thought my intentions might be, she was wrong on that count—I had no more guts to stand up to her let alone approach strange boys. I was not unaware of such things as romantic love. I was fully immersed in a rich fantasy world, shared by phantom lovers and beautiful frocks made of feathers in my summertime novels. I was unaware of the intensity of sex and knew nothing of the physical manifestations of passion. In all honestly, I was not so sure I was ready for what all the fuss was about. I sensed that such a love was a magnificent thing, and it's consummation must necessitate much toiling, waiting, and longing. I wanted to be prepared to do things the right way. I was a fourteen-year old with a mind full of acceleration and an old soul (—once again, that good friend told me so).

Anita West came on the radio as my Father turned it up. She was buzzing about the lack of zest in Van Halen's latest venture. She spoke to exactly where I was. Where nothing could electrify you more than music, more than a guitar chord struck with force and clarity. This—all of this—nature and boys of summer and righteous relatives—mattered too much. I was caught somewhere in between it all, trying to find a way out. I thought someone could relate to me; I thought that nature could comfort me. That's what I got for *thinking*.

The next day came with pursed lips and of course, long forgotten insults as we all made our way through down the cliff trail to the lake. I stood waist-high in the cool fresh water, letting small waves wash over me. They never seemed to cleanse me, to take me away with them. I never did get lost. I wondered if this feeling would ever go away? *Where have all the good times gone?*

Up the hill, we follow the trail back and the boys are seated by their cabin, a mere ten feet from the trail. I pass by them last in my virginal turquoise bikini and they whistle. They don't care if three adults are with me; they don't care that I am close enough to touch: they whistle. And it was as sweet as Eddie's guitar.

101 Ways to Die in Amsterdam

101. Drown in canal.

100. Bust ass on stairs.

99. Buy rat poison instead of coke.

98. Get creamed by over-caffeinated bicyclist.

97. Get run over by crispy motorists in extremely small cars.

96. Get smashed between train and bus.

95. Contract venereal disease by Red Light prostitute.

94. Bust ass on stairs.

93. Fall off hostel balcony, stoned.

92. WASTED.

91. Getting down with the "sunshine."

90. Go into diabetic coma trying to cop a buzz from the chocolate truffles.

89. Withdrawal.

88. Wake the neighbors.

87. Bump into the wrong person.

86. Get cleaned by street sweeper.

85. Contract rabies from hostel rat.

84. Go to jail for killing "Cigarette Cindy."

83. Consume bad falafel.

82. Get smashed between car and car.

81. Lick heroin from contaminated street.

80. Get shot by shopkeeper for taking picture of double-ended pink-jelly dong.

79. Severe head trauma from low clearance.

78. Get jacked by rowdy football fans.

77. Catch pneumonia from constant exposure to the rain.

76. Get mauled by gorillas at zoo.

75. Forget where you were going and become a vagrant.

74. Run over by train.

73. Heartbroken by recent theft due to leaving bags unattended.

72. Parasitic disease.

71. Too much reggae.

70. *Hostel* reenactment

69. Suicide

68. Pass out.